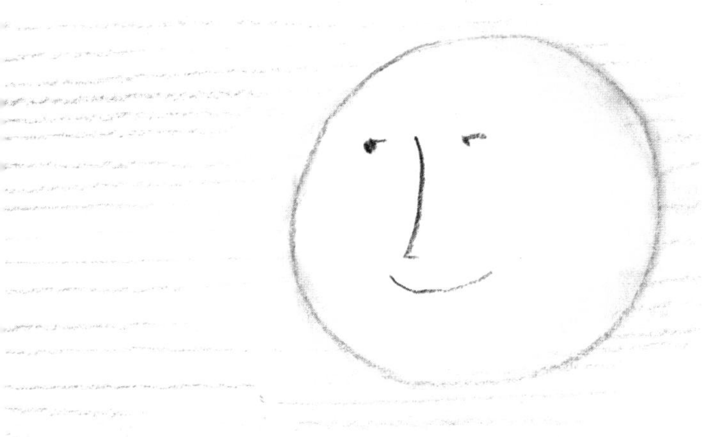

The Moon Man

a story by **Gerda Marie Scheidl**

translated and adapted by **J. Alison James**

illustrated by **Józef Wilkoń**

North-South Books
New York

Once there was a young girl named Marion who painted a picture of a Moon Man. She drew on two eyes and a nose and a cheerful smile. She drew two legs and two arms. Last, she drew a funny hat. Marion hung the picture above her bed. Now she would have moonlight even when the real moon went behind a cloud. She would have a full moon even when the real moon was just a sliver. Marion happily went to sleep.

Deep in the night, the real moon rose. It was a full moon—round and luminous. It shone through Marion's window and fell on the Moon Man.

"Atchooo!" he sneezed, and woke up.

The Moon Man took a breath, and it filled him up like a
balloon. He peeled off the page. He rolled across the floor. He
bumped down the stairs. Then he was outside in the garden.

High up in the sky the full moon shone. The Moon Man
looked up in awe. "Look at how that Moon Man glows," he said.
"If only I could shine like that!"

"Dream on," meowed a cat. "That there is the *real* moon. You
are nothing but a copy. Only the real moon can shine." The cat
yowled and tiptoed off over the rooftops.

Sadly the Moon Man walked away. He climbed up a hill that was covered in moonlight. The real moon lit up the Moon Man. Excited, he jumped up and down. "I can rub myself all over in the light, and I will shine just like the moon in the sky!" he thought.

But then the moon went behind a cloud.

Three robbers appeared out of the gloom.

"Lookee here!" they said. "The Man in the Moon has fallen out of the sky." They snatched him up. "Now we can have light whenever we need it!"

They locked the Moon Man into a glass lantern. "Shine!" they ordered. The Moon Man just smiled at them, even though he was scared. It was the only thing he knew how to do.

Suddenly the real moon came out from behind the cloud and shone in through the window.

"Ho now, wait one minute," said a robber. "You are an impostor!"

They threw the lantern on the ground, and the glass shattered. The Moon Man slipped out between the shouts of excitement.

The Moon Man came to a long silver bridge across the river. He did not know that the bridge was made of moonshine. Look out, Moon Man! The real moon went behind another cloud, and the bridge disappeared. Splash! The Moon Man fell into the water.

Fortunately a fisherman was just pulling in his nets. He thought he had caught a silver fish. When he saw the Moon Man, he was so excited, he went straight home. "Wife!" he called. "I've caught the moon!"

"It's not shining," she said. "How could it be the moon?"

The man explained. "It is just wet from falling in the river." So they hung the Moon Man out to dry and tucked him into bed.

The Moon Man pretended to sleep, but he was thinking hard. "As soon as the real moon comes out again, they will think I've gone back into the sky." He didn't want to disappoint them, so he slipped away.

The Moon Man ran and ran. He ran through a town. He ran until he came to a wall, and then he stopped.

He heard strange noises—snarling and growling and roaring. He quivered with fear. He turned to run, but it was too late!

Someone had him by the scruff of his neck. Before he knew it, he was locked in a zoo.

The Moon Man was amazed by all the animals.

"Moon! Moon!" they cried. "Shine your bright light so we can escape."

Sadly the Moon Man explained that he didn't know how to glow. But then he brightened — "I've got long thin fingers," he said. "Maybe I can unlock your cages!"

Hooting and trumpeting with glee, the animals paraded off into the hills. The Moon Man rode on the broad back of the elephant.

As they went, they discussed how to make the Moon Man shine. "The moon is bright because it is so high in the sky," said the hippopotamus. "Perhaps if the Moon Man stands on a mountain peak, he too will shine."

So the giraffe lifted the Moon Man up to the top of a tall mountain. The Moon Man smiled and thanked his new friends.

The Moon Man was happy. At last he was going to glow. He sang a cheerful little song: "Moon light, moon bright, teach me how to glow tonight!"

"Ahem," said the real moon, who was sitting on the next mountain. The real moon did not look pleased. "There can be only one moon," he said sternly. "All you have is a full-moon face, but I change each night. I go down to just a whisper—and disappear—and then come back to fill up the sky. No, there can be only one moon!"

The Moon Man felt as flat as a piece of paper. "I only wanted to shine a little," he said meekly.

"You mean you don't want to ride across the sky?"

The Moon Man shook his head.

"Well, in that case," said the real moon with a smile, "maybe I can help you."

The moon called to the Star Shiner. "Do you have some dust in your cloth from polishing stars? My friend the Moon Man wants to shine."

So the Star Shiner wrapped the Moon Man up in his dusty cloth, got on the back of a shooting star . . .

. . . and skimmed the sky until he found Marion's window. Carefully he unwrapped the Moon Man and put him back on the empty piece of paper.

The Moon Man was covered with thousands of specks of shining star dust, and he filled the room with a silvery glow.

The real moon looked in and beamed with pleasure at the Moon Man on the wall. This was the place for the Moon Man to be, right above Marion, the one who made him.

First published in the United States, Great Britain, Canada,
Australia, and New Zealand in 1994 by North-South Books,
an imprint of Nord-Süd Verlag AG, Gossau Zürich, Switzerland.
First paperback edition published in 1997.
Distributed in the United States by North-South Books Inc., New York.

Library of Congress Cataloging-in-Publication Data
Scheidl, Gerda Marie.
[Mondgesicht. English]
The Moon Man : a story / by Gerda Marie Scheidl ; translated and adapted
by J. Alison James ; illustrated by Józef Wilkon.
Summary: Marion's painting of a Moon Man comes to life and seeks ways
to shine like the real moon.
[1. Moon—Fiction. 2. Art—Fiction.] I. James, J. Alison.
II. Wilkoń, Józef, ill. III. Title.
PZ7.S3429Mo 1994 93-39759
[E]—dc20

A CIP catalogue record for this book is available from The British Library.
ISBN 1-55858-695-4 (paperback) 10 9 8 7 6 5 4 3 2 1
Printed in Belgium
For more information about our books, and the authors and artists
who create them, visit our web site: http://www.northsouth.com